Blue
Ballerina

Pink
Ballerina

Madame
Plié

Ladybird

This Little Story
belongs to

A catalogue record for this book is available
from the British Library

Published by Ladybird Books Ltd
A subsidiary of the Penguin Group
A Pearson Company
© LADYBIRD BOOKS LTD MCMXCVII

LADYBIRD and the device of a Ladybird are trademarks of
Ladybird Books Ltd Loughborough Leicestershire UK

Little
Pink Ballerina

by Ronne Randall
illustrated by Helena Owen

The little Pink Ballerina stood in front of her bedroom mirror.

"First position," she said to herself, standing tall.

"Second position," she said, holding out her arms.

The little Pink Ballerina wanted to do her very best at the Dancing School today. Madame Plié, her teacher, had promised to show the class some new steps – and the little Pink Ballerina wanted to be sure she was ready to learn them.

At the Dancing School later that morning, Madame Plié called the class to attention.

"Today I will show you how to dance like fairy princesses," she told the dancers.

"And tomorrow," she went on, "we will begin rehearsals for a special performance of *The Fairy Princess Ballet*.

"The most graceful ballerina will dance the leading part – the Star Fairy Princess."

"Ohhh!" A happy sigh went round the room.

"A fairy princess must be graceful as a feather floating through the air," Madame Plié told the dancers. "Lift your arms like this, point your toes like this, and…
whirl, twirl, leap!"

The dancers watched as Madame Plié leapt gracefully across the floor.

"Now you try," said Madame Plié.

All the dancers held up their arms and pointed their toes.

Whirl, twirl, leap! went the Blue Ballerina.

Whirl, twirl, leap! went the Yellow Ballerina.

Whirl, twirl, leap! went the Lilac Ballerina.

"Excellent!" said Madame Plié, delighted.

At last it was the Pink Ballerina's turn.

She lifted her arms, pointed her toes, and went *whirl*, *twirl*… **thump!**

"Oh, dear," said Madame Plié. "It seems that some of us haven't quite got it yet. You will have to practise very hard for tomorrow's rehearsal! Remember, dancers… graceful as a feather floating through the air!"

At home that afternoon, the Pink Ballerina practised in her room.

"*Whirl, twirl, leap!*" she said, as she lifted her arms and pointed her toes. "I'm sure I can do it!"

She started across the room.

Whirl, twirl…

thump!

"Oh, dear," said the Pink Ballerina. "Maybe I should practise in the garden. I'll have more space there."

In the garden, the birds in the cherry tree watched as the Pink Ballerina lifted her arms and pointed her toes.

"Oh, dear," sighed the little Pink Ballerina. "I'll never learn to *whirl, twirl, leap*," she whispered sadly, turning to go back into the house.

Suddenly, out of the corner of her eye, she saw something flutter down from the cherry tree.

It was a slender, silvery-white feather. The Pink Ballerina watched as it drifted gracefully through the air. And she remembered Madame Plié's words:

"A fairy princess must be graceful as a feather floating through the air…"

The Pink Ballerina picked up the silvery feather and took it inside. That night, she slept with it under her pillow and dreamt of feathers dancing gently through the clouds.

The next morning, the Pink Ballerina walked through the park with her dad, on her way to the Dancing School.

It was a lovely day, and the park was full of people. Everyone looked happy to be out in the sunshine.

Everyone, that is, except one little
boy. He was crying with all his might.
And the Pink Ballerina saw why.

The little boy's balloon was stuck in
a tree, and the string was too high
for anyone to reach.

"Don't cry!" said the Pink Ballerina, rushing up to the little boy. "I'll get your balloon!"

As a crowd gathered, the Pink Ballerina closed her eyes and thought of the silvery-white feather floating through the air.

Then she held up her arms, pointed her toes, and *whirled*, *twirled*, and... *__leapt__* as high as she could. She leapt so high that she was able to grab the balloon string, and bring the balloon safely down to the little boy.

Everyone cheered, and the little boy gave the Pink Ballerina a big thank you hug.

"I *knew* I could do it!" the Pink Ballerina thought to herself.

At the Dancing School later that morning, all the dancers were ready for the rehearsal.

Whirl, twirl, leap! went the Blue Ballerina.

Whirl, twirl, leap! went the Yellow Ballerina.

Whirl, twirl, leap! went the Lilac Ballerina.

Then it was the Pink Ballerina's turn...

As Madame Plié and all the dancers held their breath, the Pink Ballerina closed her eyes…

She thought of the silvery feather, and of that morning in the park.

Then she lifted her arms, pointed her toes, and *whirled*, and *twirled*, and **leapt** the highest, most graceful leap Madame Plié had ever seen.

"Splendid!" cried Madame Plié. "I think we have found our Star Fairy Princess!"

All the other dancers had to agree
that even though they had *whirled*
and *twirled* and *leapt* their very
best – the Pink Ballerina had given
the best performance of all. She
would be the best Star Fairy
Princess ever.

And she was!

Orange
Ballerina

Yellow
Ballerina

Lilac
Ballerina

Green
Ballerina